the Storyteller's tale

OMAIR AHMAD

SPEAKING TIGER

SPEAKING TIGER PUBLISHING PVT. LTD
4381/4, Ansari Road, Daryaganj
New Delhi – 110002

First published in English by Penguin Books 2008
First published in hardcover by Speaking Tiger 2015
This paperback edition published by Speaking Tiger 2019

ISBN: 978-93-88326-79-7

10 9 8 7 6 5 4 3 2 1

Typeset in Electra LT Regular by SÜRYA, New Delhi
Printed at R.S. Paper, Greater Noida

Omair Ahmad grew up in India and Saudi Arabia, and has worked as an analyst, reporter and political adviser in New Delhi, London and Washington. His published work includes the novels *Encounters* and *Jimmy, the Terrorist,* and a non-fiction work, *The Kingdom at the Centre of the World: Journeys into Bhutan.*

PRAISE FOR *THE STORYTELLER'S TALE*

'It isn't every day that one comes across a book that one can commend so unreservedly. Omair Ahmad's novella is a swift, elegant tale set in the badlands of Rohillakhand ... Ahmad's storyteller finds himself in a qasbah on the fringes of a haveli that soon reveals a beautiful begum. The poet is smitten, and gladly accepts an invitation to stay the night ... As befits their decorous times, they swap stories that cleverly weave in and out of each other, exploring the nuances of love and betrayal and revealing the magical power of narrative to configure and reconfigure the worlds in which we live.'—*Outlook*

'Reminiscent of the best of Indian fables, Sufi sayings and Koranic and Biblical tales. Omair Ahmad's storyteller and begum measure up to Scheherazade ... [*The Storyteller's Tale*] is a layered parable about love and sacrifice.'—*Verve*

'Using evocative prose and exquisite imagery, Omair Ahmad explores the delicate nature of human relationships, demonstrating that there is always more than one way of looking at life; that no story is ever truly finished.'—*Hindustan Times*

'[This] is perhaps as close as the printed word can get to the oral tradition... In the impassioned yet deeply personal manner of folk tales, the stories resonate with the audience as well as the readership, their philosophical and romantic underpinnings all the more poignant for being understated. Elegantly and sparsely told, epigrammatic in style, *The Storyteller's Tale* is like aged wine in a new bottle, beguiling us with complexities and surprises that challenge the core of our beliefs.'—*The Hindu*

'It's as if the same gem is turned over and over in the author's hands, the changing light showing different degrees of irradiance. In the gentle manner of narrating a folk tale, Ahmad is able to explore the valiant—yet ultimately vain—attempt to connect despite the chasm that keeps us all separate from one another... [A] compelling take on unrequited love.'—Livemint

'Ahmad, with his storytelling art, keeps his readers entranced. [His] novel does not merely entertain but gives purpose to this art.'—*Hardnews*

'[*The Storyteller's Tale*] illuminates only as stories at their purest can do.'—*First City*

For Olivia, with affection

CONTENTS

PROLOGUE

They had destroyed his house.

Ahmad Shah Abdali's men had devastated the whole of Delhi and his house had only been a small one. Its destruction would hardly have registered on the rampaging Afghans in their search for loot and pillage. It had not been a great house; only the fame of his poetry had led the noble and the rich to his door. They had been lavish with their praise, and stingy with their purses. It had meant a meagre income, a beggar's or a poet's, or that of a beggarly poet's. But his dwelling had at least kept the rain off his head, and the sun off his back.

Now he had nothing, or he had his freedom. It depended on how he looked at it, he supposed.

He had tried to find a foothold in this city. In his poetry he spoke of friendship, of love, of all those things that he would never have openly admitted to in the small town he came from. But in the many chambers of music and dance in Delhi the word 'love' was spoken of in many ways, it was nothing but a currency of exchange, of looks and glances, and promises that were never truly what they pretended to be. Here, love was a thing to be done many times.

But when he had opened his mouth to speak, the words had come out all wrong, all of them, in every which way. They had tumbled out of him, heavy with longing, wrapped in a fire that is a stranger to the light laughter of the city. The unexpectedness of speaking his own truth had stunned him.

Almost twenty years had passed, and in the end he had exactly what he had when he first arrived: his stories, his freedom and the open road before him.

THE STORYTELLER'S TALE

It was past noon when the storyteller saw the haveli. The forest path had suddenly given way to an opening and he found himself at the edge of a ridge, looking down upon the vast lawns of an estate. He could make out the stables clearly, and beyond them the tiny cluster of houses that was the sum of this casbah.

His stomach rumbled at the sight of the haveli, his body wiser than he. He had been riding for five hours now and hadn't eaten since the night before, and only lightly then. Yet, he stopped to think for a while before he went any further, dismounting from his horse and patting it awkwardly. He was not a good horseman and the horse had understood that almost instantly. Luckily he had chosen a rather placid beast, and it had borne him along well enough. It helped that he had no particular destination in mind, just the desire to put some distance between himself and those asinine traders.

He had been mildly surprised that nobody had followed; the guard whose horse he had stolen must surely have wanted it back. On the other hand these were dangerous times and there would have been little sense for the caravan to send one of its tiny contingent of guards to give chase. The thought of being even one guard short in the badlands of Rohillakhand, here where the bandits were well known to be brutally efficient at their work, would have left the fat merchants quaking in their boots.

The storyteller shook his head as the memory of the chit-chat over the last few days came back with irritating clarity. The merchants weren't scared, they were simply uncaring, and he meant nothing to them. So what if he had stolen a guard's horse and left their caravan? So what if he was the greatest poet of his age, twelve centuries after the Prophet, seventeen centuries after Christ? It meant nothing to them. Just as the destruction of their city had meant nothing more than a change of fortunes.

Ahmad Shah Abdali had led his men to devastate Delhi, destroying and looting whatever Nadir Shah, Ahmad Shah's former commander and the first man to defeat the rulers of Delhi in centuries, had left behind. The great city had been brought to its knees, and then brutalized again and again. How harsh that Ahmad Shah, a poet in the language of both the Pathans and the Persians, should be responsible for destroying this city of poets. Many of the best were dead, others scattered. Was the poet-soldier Shah Hatim still alive, the storyteller wondered, or had he laid down his life with his quill when he went, sword in hand, to the ramparts?

The memory of much of Shahjahanabad, the capital of Delhi and its empire for over five centuries, once the seat of sultans and emperors, but just debris now, refused to leave him. But these merchants, casually fleeing with their fortunes to Lucknow, seemed untouched. It had been two days since they left the city, yet the bodies of the dead, the screams of the harried still haunted the storyteller. He had sat cocooned in his grief while the traders exchanged petty gossip. One of them pestered the storyteller to indulge them with some poetry. The storyteller rebuffed the entreaties again and again, finally asking the trader what use it would be.

'It will pass the time,' the trader replied.

'It will pass your time, and destroy my words,' the storyteller answered caustically. They had withdrawn then. Maybe it had finally become apparent to them that he was not one of them, just somebody who was along on the same journey.

But it had not been enough for him. The storyteller had realized this while trying to sleep the night before. It wasn't just that he wanted to maintain a distance from them; his reputation for arrogance and impatience was enough to ensure that. There was something greater that plagued him.

A madness was upon him, he wanted to speak of the devastation that seeing the destruction of his city had caused within him. He needed to talk to somebody who would be moved by that, who would understand what beauty was, feel the pain caused by seeing beauty destroyed, a house destroyed, safety becoming nothing more than a word, the anguish of watching a child die because it had run out of a doorway just before a mounted warrior rode that way, sword bared, with a thirsty blade.

He wanted to give voice to his feelings, but he had neither the words, nor the listeners with the wit to understand them. He could have turned to the comfort of silence but the last two days had made it clear that even that would be denied to him. So he had fled, had made his way to the edge of the camp while the rest of the caravan was still gorging on a belated breakfast, stolen this horse and ridden away into the forest—ultimately to this place, overlooking this haveli, this casbah.

As the horse cropped at the grass, the storyteller untied the waterskin resting next to the saddle. He noted with wry amusement that his own bundle of goods was coming loose from where he had tied it.

So little, and even that so insecure.

Taking a mouthful of water, he rinsed the taste of dust from his mouth and swallowed. He took another sip, clean now, except for the taste of the waterskin.

The haveli had surprised him. Not because such

houses, or such habitations, were rare; but because civilization was the farthest thing from his mind just then. The Rohillas had been rising in power for the last century or so, and while it was still customary to call them 'bandits', they had become a force to be reckoned with. This haveli was probably the house of one such Rohilla noble, a descendant of Turks or Rajputs. Maybe even Pathans.

The thought that the lord of the haveli might be raiding Delhi, enriching himself on the loot that Ahmad Shah's soldiers had left behind, sickened the storyteller as he stood looking down on it. He reached out to grab the saddle and steady himself. Startled by the sudden contact, the horse turned back to look at him soulfully.

Another sip of water, smaller than before—it helped him think. He wondered whether he should avoid the casbah altogether. His sudden anger had found other things to dislike about the haveli—it was too pretty, too wealthy, too appealing. He had never had wealth, had neither begged for or inherited it, nor bought or sold for it. His pride had never allowed him to write verses in praise of petty nobles so that they would allow him to eat well, to wear bright clothes and fix gems into his turban.

It was a stupid thing for a poet, for a storyteller, to have his pride. After all, where would an artist receive wealth from if not the rich? And who, if not the wealthy, could put a value to beauty? He was no Sufi who could sing his verses at a shrine, relying on the grace of God and the petty contributions of thousands of unwashed hands to feed him. And yet he had never been able to let it go—this pride, this distrust, this unwillingness to bend. He had mocked himself countless times, most famously with the couplet that was now so intimately tied to his own name: '*Sar kisi se firoh nahin hota; haif bande hue, khuda na hue.*' The head does not bow before any other; the tragedy is that I was born a man, and not a god.

Like many others, the storyteller had made a morality out of his own disability. Since he couldn't make poems praising the rich and powerful, he despised those who could. But he could have done things other than being a poet, or moving along the alleyways of Delhi telling his stories. There was no reason for him to become a storyteller except for his love of beauty, and his passion to share it.

Once, before he made his way to Delhi, he had worked with steel and wood. His father had died when he was still quite young, and he had become an apprentice to his uncle next door, an artisan famous for his skill. The storyteller had enjoyed making things, especially pretty things. It had given him peace. People had paid him—sometimes compliments, sometimes food, and sometimes even money. Barely a teenager then, it had been enough for him.

His customers kept the beauty he created for them, but not always in the way he would want. Once, a man had broken the leg of a chair and beaten his wife to death with it. She had been the one to commission that chair from the storyteller, and he had put his heart into carving the designs onto the wood for the sake of her lovely, mocking eyes. He had seen the dried blood on the chair leg two days after the murder, and decided that he would no longer make beautiful things of substance; only beauty out of words.

He could have chosen to detach himself from beauty altogether, but he didn't. It was hypocrisy of a kind to create one type of beauty and distrust others, and he knew it. Nor was he so naïve as to think that words were safe. He was aware of their dangers but he could always deny his role in what happened afterwards. Words are just flowers, he told himself. They will wither and die after I am gone, but they will be beautiful when I gift them.

The storyteller stood gazing at the haveli, unsure of what to do, when he saw a figure suddenly appear and make its way to the stables. Despite the distance that separated them, he could tell it was a woman, and that she was beautiful.

His decision was made for him.

And isn't that the sum of all love? The whole story of love? Something that takes you by surprise, something that is seen from a distance, and yet recognized instantly and clearly? Something you are scared of your whole life long, and yet, when faced by it, reach for with open arms?

And isn't that the story of folly, the sum of it? Fools who see mirages in the desert and convince themselves they are real, who fall in love with ideas and illusions, give their whole hearts up to them, and blame reality when it intrudes?

But nobody saw or heard the storyteller's thoughts. They were like the wind over the wasteland, giving neither relief nor wisdom.

By the time the three-man retinue rushed out to guard the woman as she made her way to the stables, the storyteller had already mounted his startled steed and persuaded it down the ridge towards the haveli.

The woman didn't seem to notice the storyteller until he was close enough to see that he was right about her beauty. More surprisingly her guards, too, noticed him quite late and hurriedly arranged themselves in a protective triangle facing him. The captain raised his voice, ordering the storyteller to stop. It was only then that the woman looked in his direction, and paused. The storyteller did not halt his horse, and there really was no point in slowing it down as it was moving at a very leisurely pace to begin with.

Before the guards could tell him to halt again there was a shrill squawk from the haveli and a scrawny old man holding a parasol came rushing out. Emerging behind him was a round, middle-aged hen of a woman, brandishing a stick. Her voice carried clearly across the distance, 'Lazy, good-for-nothing son of misbegotten goats! Curse the moment when I married you, whose blood is unsure and bones carry the traces of who knows which clan. You can't even remember to provide shade for the Begum! Ya Allah, what will the Mirza say when he comes back to find his wife all shrivelled and brown?'

The scuttling man with the parasol seemed to be propelled along by the very power of his wife's insults. A few of the words appeared to be directed at the Begum as well, but she just shook her head. Meanwhile the others watched the progress of husband and wife, till the old man brought the parasol to rest above the Begum's head, saving her delicate skin from the sun, and himself from his wife's wrath. It was then that the guards raised their muskets and once again ordered the storyteller to stop.

'Declare yourself. Who are you to enter, unannounced, the property of Mirza Azeem Jalal-ud-din Khan?'

'A storyteller,' he answered, and dismounted clumsily.

The guards seemed confused by his answer, but the Begum turned to look at him. The parasol covered her face, so he could not see her expression. Nor would it have been wise to stare at her. Prudently he kept his gaze on the soldiers instead. Nevertheless he noticed the Begum raise an elegant hand and summon her maid, who stopped mid-curse and quickly made her way to her mistress' side.

Their conversation took place in hushed tones and then the maid forced her way through the soldiers and asked the storyteller, 'My Begum would like to know which city you belong to.'

The storyteller couldn't help himself; the words just spilled out, '*Dilli, jo ek shahr tha, aalam mein intekhaab/ Rahte the muntakhab hi jahaan rozgaar ke/ Jisko falakh ne loot kar barbaad kar diya/ Hum rahnewale hain usi ujde dayaar ke.*' Delhi, that chosen city of the world/ Where only those of privileged professions resided/ That the heavens have looted and laid waste/ I am an inhabitant of that destroyed garden.

His words fell upon the others like an unexpected assault. He saw the maid's arrogance dip, the guards' muscles ease, and the parasol waver in the grip of the old man only to straighten once again. And he saw the Begum raise her eyes towards his and freeze until he had spoken the last lingering syllable.

The words swept the area clean, leaving a silence in their wake, a new reality. A new world where it was no longer improper for him to stare directly at the Begum, and he drank in her beauty in the moments he had. It seemed that she owned black; the dark richness of her hair shaping her face in the same way that the kohl marked out her eyes. Her razor sharp features appeared to cut the wind around her, making it bleed for mercy.

For a moment the tableau held, and then she blinked, long lashes hiding those eyes. A few soft words were exchanged between mistress and servant, and the maid came haughtily to the storyteller to say, 'The Begum asks if you will rest on your way and share your stories with us. The Mirza and his Begum are known for their generosity.'

The storyteller bowed, 'It shall be my honour.'

Within moments one of the guards grabbed the reins of the storyteller's horse, while another removed the badly tied bundle behind the saddle. The Begum had started on her way back to the stables, and the rest followed her, including the guard leading the storyteller's horse. Only the one hefting the bundle remained behind with the storyteller. 'Come,' he said.

The storyteller followed the guard to the pretty, rich building that he had looked upon with such mistrust only a short while ago.

'Where does your Begum go?' the storyteller finally asked.

'Riding,' the guard grunted in exasperation. 'Riding in Rohillakhand, while the Mirza and his men are abroad and we are too few to guard her properly. But she will not listen. It is the Pathan blood; it hasn't cooled even after generations of living in this land. The Mirza was warned when he wanted her for a wife, but he is a headstrong man, and without his parents to curb his impetuosity, none can thwart his will.'

And so I am in the house of my enemies, the

storyteller thought, *and they shall be generous to me from what they have looted from my neighbours, from the wealth of destroyed houses and broken lives*.

Now that the Begum and her beauty were gone, the memory of those eyes already fading, the storyteller felt lost and confused. A sudden sense of panic washed over him and he realized he didn't know what he was doing. *I should run away*, he thought, *I should disappear. Now, before anything more is done.*

But he was a storyteller, and he had said he would tell a story. He would keep his word. The story that he would tell rose within him; he felt the words, spoke them soundlessly as he rediscovered the tale, felt its texture as it emerged. By the evening, when he had bathed and eaten, when the Begum had come back from her long ride, the storyteller knew the tale he would tell.

You will forgive me, (the storyteller began, addressing the Begum's maid that evening, in the grand hall where the Begum reclined on a divan, while her maid washed and oiled her hands to make sure they remained soft and beautiful, despite their obvious unwomanly strength) if I tell you a story told among villages, and poor people. Love is not exclusive to high places, or those of noble birth. It is sometimes more easily observed among those who have no need to hide behind custom and fear of dishonour.

There was a forest and around it were villages. The forest had many stories, as did the villages. One such story began with the unwed daughter of a village headman.

She committed an act. A sin, the villagers called it, but whether it was a sin of lust, of love or of folly, they did not know for she refused to tell them about it. Thus her sin was compounded in their eyes by the sin of silence. All the village knew was that she was going to have a child but they did not know whether to condemn her or console her, and seemingly content in her crime, she would not let them know either.

Her shamelessness was not to be borne, the women declared. And if there was jealousy and confusion in them, it only made them sure about what they said.

Her shamelessness was not to be borne, the men agreed. And if, behind their solemn tones, there was shame and incomprehension, they did not let it show.

Her mother was long dead. Her father only looked at her; neither asking her to speak, nor demanding that she should do so. So the villagers condemned him, too, the anger in their voices rising every night around the fire where the decisions were taken. Every night the flames leapt higher.

Yet, though they condemned her, they could not forget that she was one of their own. Despite all their criticism, all their anger and all their confusion, some of them were kind to her. The women remembered the joy they had shared with her when they had played as children, and recalled too her strength and her strangeness. But when the baby's first cries were heard in the village, the men could take it no longer.

'Is our honour so cheap that we can let a bastard thrive amongst us?' they said.

'Will that child of sin play with our children, and stain them with the crime he was born from?'

'Will we have to explain to strangers that a bastard can be born from one of our women and we have neither the courage to find out who the father is, nor the strength to punish him?'

And so the voices rose again, and somebody said, 'Kill the child.'

Nobody knew who said it first, but once it was spoken, it became everyone's decision. And though the men lacked the strength to speak of it to their wives as their own decision, they defended it as that of their brothers.

The father of the unwed mother, the grandfather of the fatherless child, who had said nothing and asked no questions, went to his hut. Taking a sharp axe, a knife, some fishhooks, a little rope and some flint, he went to his daughter, who was feeding her newborn, and she understood what was meant.

Neither of them wept.

So it was that the woman was walking deep in the woods when the men burst into her father's hut to find her and the child, the sign of their shame, gone from the village. But violence cannot be denied; they had broken the thin shell that kept them human, and now were neither animals nor men. They saw the old man looking at them, and found something in his eyes that had been there in his daughter's.

Nobody claimed the first blow; afterwards, everybody denied remembering who it was that had raised his hand initially. It matters little now; what matters is that at the end of it the old man was dead, his hut ablaze, and the next day the men slunk back to their lives.

The village never spoke of their shame again.

And so it was that the woman was walking deep in the woods, when she felt an intense sadness rise in her, a bone-weary tiredness, and she could no longer continue. She sat down with her little bundle—the last gifts from her father and a few things of her own—and wept for all that was gone.

As her tears subsided she heard faint whimpering nearby. It was not her baby, who slept peacefully, but some other creature, not human but . . . Suddenly, it became vital for her to find the creature, and she searched frantically in the weak light of the false dawn until she found the source.

In the bushes were three dead bodies, and one

living one. A she-wolf had died, and around it were the bodies of two of her cubs. A third cub was still alive. Looking up at the woman, it bared its teeth and growled in warning. As she came closer, it backed away, whether to protect its mother's dead body or seek shelter from it was unclear.

The woman, who was still overcome by her grief, took out her breast that had more milk than her baby needed, and squeezed some out on a cloth before offering it to the cub. Hunger won over distrust and the cub came to suckle at the wet cloth wrapped around her finger. When it was dry he growled and nipped at her finger, pleading.

The woman looked up at the trees, and spoke to the forest. 'I accept.'

She raised the cub with her son, as another son, but only for a year.

In the wilderness she thought to name her son Taka, which meant Nameless in her language. She wanted him to be free, to be without any fetters or bonds, not even those of a name. But the baby was a generous one, and when he first spoke the name Taka, he meant his brother, the wolf cub.

It was then that the mother began to distrust the cub, for in his love her son had given the cub what she would have liked him to have. In her heart something was born. It was small at first, but grew a little every day. She called her son Wara—free—but she couldn't find a name for that feeling that rose in her heart. She hadn't hated before.

A year passed since the woman entered the forest, and it treated her well. She made a small home for herself by a lake filled with fish. She taught herself to make bows and arrows, and although her first experiments were failures, by the end of her first year she managed to kill a deer.

But her son had given his name to the cub, and it gnawed at her, and she grew mistrustful of the forest. She looked at Taka, who had grown so quickly and was almost his full size, and thought of how much he ate. She grew resentful of how hard she worked to provide for him. When she left the cub and the baby alone now, she tied the cub to a tree, not trusting him. On her return, she called to her son Wara, who was free, and held him close before patting Taka on his head, and releasing him.

Neither the child minded, nor did the cub understand. They had known only love and were too young to measure affection or the lessening of it. They couldn't compare how their mother treated them. Besides, it was with each other that they spent most of their time—laughing, playing or curled up asleep. Even when Taka was tied to his place, Wara went to him, so there were times when the woman came back to see bite marks on Wara's arms and legs.

Wara didn't mind—he bit Taka too—but in his mother's heart the fear grew each day and she took to tying Taka with a stronger rope, twined from the vines she found.

As her heart grew colder it seemed that the forest did too. That year there were fewer fish and game was hard to find. Taka was hungry as always; he was almost two years old and full grown but the woman started to feed him less so that she could save food for herself and Wara.

One day in late winter, she tied Taka to a tree and, carrying her axe, left in search of food. The wolf tried to lick her face and hands, but she pushed him away, irritated. The sound of childish laughter and delighted exclamations of 'Taka, Taka, Taka,' followed her as she walked deeper into the woods.

She found little that day, and moved further and further away from home. Late in the evening and far from home, a sudden feeling of foreboding overwhelmed her—Wara was in danger. Flinging away the roots she had gathered, she turned back towards the lake, and ran. She was far away from her son, and it took her time to reach him, time enough for fear to destroy the little love that was left and leave only hate.

It had been a hard and hungry winter. Animals that generally did not live in the forest had found their way there, famished and in search of food. Three wild dogs, all that was left of their pack, had entered the forest. Hungry and fearless, the pack had attacked a tiger over his kill. The king of the forest had warned them away with his thunderous roars but they were too ravenous to know fear. The tiger had killed and killed again, mowing them down ruthlessly until he had been torn down himself. These three had survived that holocaust that killed more than a dozen of their kin. They had gorged themselves, until they were forced to move again.

They heard Wara and Taka from a distance, the child's voice sweetly tempting. They weren't scared of the wolf. They had fought bigger creatures, and their hunger was a living thing, more real than they.

Taka scented them first, a strange but familiar smell, like the reek of an evil cousin. He barked at Wara, but the child didn't understand. Taka barked more insistently, but the child kept running further away. It was a new game they had developed. Wara knew that Taka could only chase him as far as the rope would let him, so he remained just out of Taka's reach.

Taka was straining at the rope when he saw the first wild dog emerge from the bushes. The wolf retreated a few steps and lunged, hoping to break the rope, but it was strong and well tied. Wara turned back to look at his brother and fell.

The other two dogs reached the clearing as well, mystified by the unfamiliar scents—they hadn't hunted humans before. One of them approached the child, and sniffed. It was only then that Wara realized what Taka had been barking at. He was unafraid; he had fought Taka who was much bigger than the wild dogs. Wara hit the dog on the snout with his fist. The creature reared back in surprised pain and then lunged to bite. Wara was quick but the teeth tore into his soft skin and his blood shone in the sunlight. The moment was enough to break the stillness of the other two dogs. The smell of the blood told them that the child was exactly what they had been looking for—food. They attacked, afraid that the first dog would leave nothing behind.

It was this that saved Wara. As the dogs tumbled over each other he ran towards Taka who had been straining against the rope in frustration and fear. He was full grown now; the rope had only held him before this because he hadn't tried to break free with any great effort. Now he didn't care that the rope tore through his fur, that it coloured him with his own blood. He lunged again and again.

Wara fell before he could reach the safety of Taka's shadow but Taka had broken free by then to save his brother.

The dogs hesitated. Better fed and angry, Taka was twice as large as any of them. But their hunger was a madness of the brain, and they had killed a tiger before. The one that had already tasted blood lunged first.

It was Taka's first real battle and he didn't know how to manoeuvre. The dogs had been fighting their whole lives long and were sly with it. They nipped and tore at him, keeping just out of reach of his massive jaws. And if he moved to attack, they lunged at Wara.

The fight went on for a long time and the hunger that was driving the dogs was weakening them too, and one of them slipped. Before he could recover Taka had him by the throat and it took only one powerful bite to break the dog's neck. The two survivors hesitated, and then one of them lunged.

But Taka was a wolf now, a wolf that had made its first kill. He swatted the second dog in the middle of its leap and tore into its stomach, ripping out its life. The third dog tried to run but it was alone, and with no one to distract him, Taka took only a moment to make the kill.

He howled then, howled his bloodlust and his joy. And the woman, who had run through the forest, heard him. Her heart failed her and she knew without it being explained to her that it was the sound of a wolf that had tasted blood.

'Wara!' she cried, and Taka heard her.

He ran then to tell his mother of how he had saved his brother, to show her that he had grown up, had become what he was meant to be. He ran to his mother to tell her of his love, and to be loved in turn.

She saw the blood on his jaws, his slavering tongue, the gleam in his eyes; she saw a wolf. With a swing of her axe, with all the power she could summon, she killed the wolf.

'Oh, how you have betrayed me!' she cried.

The lamps had burned low by the time the storyteller ended his story. There was a sudden snuffling sound as the old man, the husband of the Begum's maid, tried to stifle sudden tears. The maid glared at her husband till he quieted and then turned back to stare at the storyteller.

A discreet gesture and the maid rose ponderously to attend to the Begum. She nodded at the words whispered into her ears and then turned towards the storyteller, a look of grim satisfaction on her face as she said, 'My lady says that you know betrayal very well, storyteller, and of the giving of pain to those of generous hearts. She asks when you will be on your way.'

Behind her the Begum's mouth was set, and unexpected lines had appeared around her mouth.

'Where will you be off to next?' the maid asked, each word hard.

The question should have hurt the storyteller, for, as after the telling of every tale, his heart was open and he was defenceless. But he was too tired.

He couldn't feel the pain.

THE BEGUM'S REPLY

It was past noon when she saw him. It had been one of those days when she was convinced that somebody was coming, that at last a breath of fresh air would come rushing in and disturb her life. The Mirza was gone, and without him she felt her imprisonment that much more keenly. There was so little she could do in this place, so much nothing. Her blood was not the quiet thing that was expected in these parts, but a powerful surging energy, and confined in this haveli all it could do was to batter her. Sometimes she felt she would go mad from the raging within her.

Why was it that the Mirza could ride to war, could lead men to battle, and hold them by the fine leash of their loyalty to him while she remained trapped here? Whoever heard of a hawk that became a dove after mating? He had asked for her hand because of the stories of her fire, and now he would have her live as his pet. It was a cruel thing he did, one of the many he enjoyed here, in Rohillakhand, where he was master.

Her loneliness had drawn her to the window in the room that faced the forest, the room that was not her own, but became so when the Mirza was gone. It was the only place in the haveli where she could escape the pettiness of the casbah. Although she detested the weakness in herself that longed for company, that told her that she was not complete in herself, she sat down at the table to look out.

Thus it was that she saw him emerge from the forest, turbaned and bewildered, lost and inelegant, a wild creature happening unexpectedly upon the edges of civilization. She blinked, but he didn't disappear. She blinked again, and still he stood there, upon the ridge. She watched him dismount clumsily and almost laughed at the way he patted the horse. Even from a distance she could imagine the fond disgust of the steed for its master. Then he turned towards the haveli, and she found she couldn't breathe. It was only after long moments that she let a breath escape, whistling softly over her tongue. This was no illusion. She forgave her heart for lying to her so many times before. Its prophecy had been true; it was just she who had been impatient, who had turned her longing into disappointment. Wrapping her arms around herself she watched contentedly as this visitor looked upon her life.

He stiffened then, almost as if he had become aware of her regard at the moment she had sighed. She saw him turn his head, cocking it slightly as though in thought. It was a familiar gesture, reminding her of the deer she had seen on her hunts, who had stood, heads cocked to the side and one hoof raised, deciding whether to run or not upon detecting her presence. It delighted her to see this man do the same thing.

The soft smile that curved the corners of her mouth wasn't enough to express her joy and she laughed, a low, throaty sound that warmed the cold room, spreading through the haveli. She liked him already, this stranger, this sudden friend who hadn't even arrived yet. Out on the ridge the man reached for the waterskin tied behind his saddle, took a sip and stood, contemplating. She wondered at his thoughts: Did he like the haveli? Was he intimidated by its grandeur, or touched by its beauty? Did he understand the effort it had taken to make this haveli into something more than just a fortress; something beautiful as well as grand, a warm welcome in this corner of the world? She was gripped by impatience and panic as she watched him hesitate.

A friend has to be welcomed, she reasoned and he was, at the very least, a friend. Hadn't he made her smile, made her laugh?

She got up and made her way to the door. Mehrunnisa, her maid, would be angry. She saw Mehrunnisa's husband asleep by the door and didn't waste time trying to wake him, to explain that she was going to the stables, to ride again. He would only whine and plead, the fear of the Mirza in his rheumy eyes, and she would feel the trap close in on her.

The minute she stepped out of the haveli she was suddenly buffeted by the full force of the moment. In the distance she could feel the stranger mount his horse that would bring him inevitably to the haveli, like the slow sliding of a few pebbles before an avalanche. Behind her she heard the call from one of the guards, and somewhere behind her Mehrunnisa's voice rose in surprised annoyance.

Ignoring everything, she made her way to the stables. And even though she had seen him from the distance, had taken the one step outside of the haveli that would draw him like a magnet to her, even though she had tasted Fate itself in the air, his presence took her by surprise. It was a good thing, this surprise of hers. It made them equals in a way. There was no lie in her voice when she turned to see the guards confront him. She could ignore him, as manners dictated, and let the guards handle the first stage of the encounter, only stepping in when it was obvious that her command was necessary.

But even then she was not truly prepared for him to say that he was a storyteller, with all the hauteur of a petty magician. She was even less prepared for the poetry that rolled off his tongue, became something grand, hurting, and real. She heard his voice as it strained under the load of its love for a city that her husband was raiding; she heard his heartbreak and was trapped. This time it was she who froze like a deer unexpectedly sighting a hunter.

It was a good thing, this fear that he brought with him. She could not be seen to accept him openly, to welcome him to the haveli. There needed to be distance, and his words provided that. She needed to get away, needed time to ride his words out of her blood.

So she asked Mehrunnisa to invite him to tell a story, and made her way to the stables. Her mare whinnied to see her, and she fed the beast a lump of sugar from the store at the stable, pleased with its welcome. She turned then to where her bow was stored, drawing it forth and restringing it. The ritual tightened her muscles and something about the bent bow, the thrumming of the bowstring delighted her. It seemed that the vibrating bowstring and the tense bow were filled with the same sense of suppressed excitement as she was. By this time more of the guards had arrived, so that when she left the grounds, half-a-dozen men and the complaining Mehrunnisa rode alongside her.

The Begum tried to keep her pace slow, but the mare felt the tension and pulled at the bit, striking out at speed through the forest, until the Begum, much against her own will, brought the steed back into control. Thus it was that the party, caught between sudden spurts of speed and periods of control, burst forth upon a glade in the late afternoon. There was a herd of deer unexpectedly present, a few drinking from the stream, and others leisurely cropping the grass. One stag stood in stately authority overseeing the rest. As the rest of the herd scrambled to its feet or fled, he stood his defiance.

The Begum had not meant to hunt but the bow appeared naturally in her hands. Still, the stag had an opportunity to flee while the hunting party came to a stop and the Begum steadied her hands, but it stayed, hesitating. As the Begum nocked an arrow to the bowstring the stag raised one hoof and turned, but it was much too late. As it rose on its haunches in its first great leap the arrow had already left the bow. Before the whole of her breath had been released, the Begum saw the arrow strike, driving deep inside.

Mortally wounded, the stag made a futile attempt

to reach the safety of the trees. The Begum saw it take one last leap, stagger and fall as its legs gave way underneath it. Her guards were already rushing past her, their knives out, and a sick feeling came rising up from her stomach. She had not ridden out to kill, and yet it had all come so naturally. The great beast was sprawled on the ground, its life almost gone. Men dismounted quickly around it, and while two of them held it down, another cut open its throat in the ritual fashion, saying a few brief words to a distant God as the bright blood pooled in the dirt at their feet.

The Begum's mare brought her to the fallen beast but she could barely recognize it now. All the vitality had fled. The proud head lolled to its side, and the shiny coat was caked with dust and blood. A few muscles quivered in its flanks, the last faint twitches of a flight begun too late.

A sudden sadness came over the Begum, and she turned away, hiding her emotion from the men. She could not be seen to be weak, and said, roughly, 'Keep its heart for me.'

There was a sharp intake of breath from

Mehrunnisa who had arrived only in time to witness the death and the Begum's words.

'Eating another's heart hardens one's own,' the maid said.

The words roused the Begum to sudden, swift anger. 'It is your superstition, not mine,' she said. 'Among our people it is a mark of respect.' She had truly not meant to kill that day and this was all she could do to weaken the load of this unexpected death upon her conscience.

Her men were efficient, and in a few minutes the stag had been lifted and tied to one of the horses. Their return journey was much slower, given that the smell of the blood made the horses skittish. Even the Begum's mare seemed to feel the mood and curtailed its excitement.

Back at the haveli, some of the Begum's joy came back to her after she bathed. She had a guest, a storyteller, someone who had already made her smile and laugh today and she hoped his words would ease away the pain of the stag's death. When she sat down on her divan with her maids around her, she was eager and willing to be entertained. But something was wrong from the moment the storyteller entered the room—he came as somebody both haughty and humbled, a king before his executioners. And his words were bitter indeed.

The story he told was of love, and the hurt, fear and distrust that come when love remains unrecognized. He told the story well, as if he had come to know the many flavours of suffering intimately over time. She thought it ill done of him to return her kindness and welcome with such pain when she had regarded him as a friend, and had invited him into her home. She called to Mehrunnisa, and made her displeasure plain.

'And where will you be off to next?' Mehrunnisa asked, each word full of her mistress' intent to hurt. The Begum saw the storyteller blink and pretend that there was no pain. The gesture reached past the defences she had been drawing around herself, and melted her. She realized that the storyteller had hurt her out of fear that he would be rejected where he had been welcomed—and in that fear he had hurt her enough that she rejected him.

Why were men such fools, that they created the very hurts for themselves that they most feared?

She spoke as he started to rise, to hold him, teach him a lesson in manners, 'Would you like to listen to a story in return?'

The words were not addressed to him for she could not address a stranger thus. Finding himself the sudden focus of the Begum's eyes, Afzal, Mehrunnisa's husband, trembled. 'Begum, of course, but we have never heard you tell a story before . . .'

She laughed harshly then, laughed at them all. 'What, is it such a hard thing to tell a tale that only penniless wanderers can tell them? Is the Mirza's wife of such little worth that she cannot do what an indigent poet can do?'

Out of the corner of her eye she saw the storyteller blush at her mockery. He could assert his special skill, or welcome this humiliation he so richly deserved. She saw him struggle with himself, and say nothing. That was good.

What a child he is, she thought, how like children all men are.

'Listen, Afzal mian,' she said, 'listen closely, for this is a story from my homeland where men have broken open mountains to win their beloved's hand, where death is a small price for loyalty, and where a brother is a brother . . . ever and always.'

There was once an empire. Its name is not important for it changed hands many times. But among its borderlands was a place called Thakir that kept its name, no matter who ruled. The Amir of Thakir was a powerful man, one of the great defenders of the empire from the rampaging hordes that lived to the west of the border. An intelligent man of great feeling, he had the fortune to find a wife who was his equal, a partner with whom the world became more truly itself, and he threw himself into his work and his love as few men ever had.

In time the Amir and his wife had a son, and they named him Aresh, which means 'generosity', for they were happy with what had been given to them and took their gifts from life graciously. Perhaps they named him truly, for Aresh marked the sum of life's generosity to them. The Amir's wife never recovered from the weakness of childbirth, and passed away within a few months. The Amir was heartbroken, and for all the love he had lavished on his wife, he found he had little left for his son. He cherished the child, but his wife's death had robbed him of something important and he could no longer reach out to people.

It was at the same time that a maid, who worked in the palace, also gave birth to a son. In the natural course of things she would have wet-nursed the Amir's son, but the Amir wanted more than that. He summoned the maid and her husband, a woodcutter, and told them to bring their baby with them.

The couple came at the appointed hour, trembling in fear. The Amir was a powerful man, and they had been beneath his notice until then. Moreover, the grimness that had descended upon him since his wife's death had been the topic of much conversation in the palace halls.

'I would like to see your child,' the Amir said. As these words left the Amir's mouth, the woman started wailing and collapsed into a teary heap. Despite the knowledge of his own powerlessness, the woodcutter rose to defend his family. 'Sire,' he said, twisting his cap in his hands, 'we know of your grief, but please . . . don't punish us for our joy.'

The Amir watched the scene unfold with wry amusement. 'Speak!' he commanded. 'No man here will harm you. What is it that you fear?'

The woodcutter was unconvinced, and lowered his head in response.

'Speak!' the Amir's voice rang throughout the court, bringing the woodcutter to attention.

'We feared . . .' the woodcutter began, then swallowed, continuing in a low voice that could barely be heard, 'we feared for our lives and that of our child. We feared you would punish us for being happy in your time of grief.'

The Amir laughed then, but grimly, 'No. I haven't fallen so low. I had but a favour to ask of you and your wife.'

'Sire . . .?'

'My son needs a wet nurse now that he has lost his mother, but I wouldn't have summoned you if that was all that he needed,' the Amir said. 'He has been deprived of much more than that. He needs a mother; he needs a family, and a brother. I would have you raise him along with your son, but both boys will be taught and trained in the palace. It is an honour that I would give you, on the condition that you can bring up my son in the manner befitting him, and your son in a manner appropriate for my son's closest companion.'

The other people at the court were too stunned to respond, but then one of them ventured, 'My lord, perhaps a more suitable family . . .'

But the Amir raised his hand, and the speaker fell silent.

'Tell me,' the Amir turned to the woodcutter, 'will you do this?'

It was the maid who responded, 'We will do this, Sire.'

'Good,' the Amir nodded. 'Now bring me your son, that I may give him a name that will be worthy of him.'

The woodcutter was quiet for the couple had already named their son. Again it was the wife who spoke, raising the bundle she had been holding, 'This is not my son, Sire.'

One of the soldiers moved towards the maid, and remarked, 'Sire, it is only a bundle of clothes.'

The Amir laughed, 'At least you are brave.'

So it was that the woodcutter's son was named Barab, which means 'pillar' and he became the closest friend, the 'brother' with whom Aresh spent his childhood. The Amir was right when he had said that Aresh would need more than a wet nurse in Thakir. As the Amir's only child, he had no equals and everybody wished to be in the Amir's favour. Only Barab was free from motive, and when he hit Aresh it was because he thought of Aresh as his brother, and when he stole sweets from the kitchen for Aresh he expected nothing more than his brother's delight.

The woodcutter often played with the boys, and though his fear of the Amir was too great for him to be completely at ease, he taught them how to whittle toys out of wood. He made them their first knives, and carved for them their first walking sticks. He meticulously taught them the names of all the trees and bushes in the woods, which berries and fruits were good to eat and which were not. But as they grew older, the woodcutter saw his future master in Aresh, and became even meeker than he should have been.

The maid, however, had less fear. She had cleaned the child, and fed him; had dealt with his vomit and his illnesses. She had kissed him on the stomach to make him smile, and tried to catch him as he ran naked through the house, laughing like the child he was.

It was Barab who paid the greatest price. He could have grown up as just another child in Thakir, but that was denied him. Nor did he enjoy the respect that was accorded to Aresh; even his own parents treated him with less care than what they showed Aresh, though with as much love. He didn't have the fine clothes Aresh had and nobody bowed to him. One day, when they had come into their adolescence, Barab looked at his rough garments and those of Aresh, and said, 'We can't be friends.'

'Why do you say that?' Aresh asked, barely able to keep the hurt out of his voice.

'Look at us, Aresh. You are the Amir's only son and my father is a humble woodcutter. You will have your wealth, your fine clothes and your power. I will always struggle to keep up with you, and I will always fail.'

Aresh thought about what Barab had said, and then grinned, 'This is about that girl, isn't it? The one who is visiting the castle with her family?'

At that Barab blushed furiously, because his brother was right.

Aresh hooted with laughter, 'Oooh! Barab is in love!'

'Shut up!' Barab grumbled and took a swipe at Aresh.

But Aresh was enjoying himself far too much to stop. 'Barab is in love with Little-Princess-I-Am-Very-Fine!' he teased. Barab tried to catch him, but Aresh evaded his grasp. In the end Barab gave up, and grumpily sat down to pluck at the grass.

'Why don't you sneak into her room?' Aresh suggested from a safe distance. 'Then you can declare your love for her?'

Barab blushed again, but he asked, 'Do you really think I could?'

'I'll help you,' Aresh said. 'You can even borrow my clothes.'

At that Barab shook his head. He was much larger than Aresh, and wouldn't have fitted into his clothes.

Like many childhood escapades, it came to nothing in the end. When the girl's caravan returned to Yasurat, the capital of the empire, Barab was dejected and broken-hearted, but his friendship with Aresh was stronger than ever. They came to laugh about it, and devised increasingly complicated plans to woo the next beautiful girl who came to stay at the palace.

But Yasurat entered their lives in a wholly unexpected way.

Not long after Aresh had celebrated his seventeenth birthday, his father summoned him. As usual, Barab came along with him, but it was to Aresh that the Amir spoke first.

'You have grown up well, my son,' the Amir began, 'and I'm proud of the young man you have become. But you have reached the end of the education that Thakir can give you.'

Aresh said nothing.

'You will rule, one day, either in these lands or others,' the Amir continued. 'But here, in Thakir, you already do; people bow to you, but you have yet to earn their respect. Soon people will petition you, but you lack the experience to understand whether they ask for good things or bad. I have arranged for you to go and work with a friend of mine, in Yasurat. He is a magistrate in the city, and an important man. You will be his assistant. It's not a small position and he is not an easy man to please; you will have to work hard to earn your place.'

The Amir then turned to Barab, 'In all the things of youth you have been Aresh's companion, and a fine one. But your paths cannot be the same. Were you brothers in blood your paths would still diverge one day—the elder son rules and the younger protects, that is how our world works. When Aresh leaves, you will join the army that defends these borders.'

And with that the Amir dismissed them.

On the day that Aresh left, Barab rode with him a little way along the road to Yasurat, and as they were parting he said, 'Aresh, we always knew that such a parting would come. Should I say goodbye to you now? We have been friends throughout our childhood, and I have been given a greater share of life than was my due. Our futures will be different though, and I'd rather part ways now than let our company become difficult for each other.' And though it was unmanly to do so, Barab wept and asked, 'Tell me, should I say farewell?'

Aresh gripped his friend's hand in a strong clasp, and replied, 'Barab, you have been truer to me than most brothers are. I won't cast away the dearest friend I have for fear of what may happen in the future.'

But Barab was the woodcutter's son, not the Amir's, and he was unsure. 'Promise me, then,' he demanded, 'that two years from now we will meet again at this place.'

'I promise,' Aresh vowed, and they parted.

It took Aresh a month to reach Yasurat, and he was amazed by the city. He had never visited it before, and its size and bustle were like nothing he had ever experienced. It became apparent very soon that here he would be treated like everybody else; nobody paid any special attention to him, or made way for him, and for the first time in his life he felt insignificant. But this was only his perception. He rode a noble horse, and bore all the hallmarks of wealth and power. People noticed the way he carried himself, with the natural confidence of a man of power. A few bowed in respect, and he returned the gesture, mistaking it for common courtesy. Here in Yasurat, however, few people merited such attention. Those who observed him and his retinue, and noted that he was somebody important, weren't surprised when he made his way to the magistrate's house where he was greeted with great respect.

Aresh was in awe at such a welcome and when, after bathing and making himself presentable, he joined the magistrate and his wife for dinner, he felt like a clumsy country oaf, far out of his depth. The magistrate was cool and polite, his face revealing nothing of his thoughts, and his young wife was beautiful and enigmatic. They asked him several questions, and he answered as truthfully as he could. He was conscious of his inexperience, and spoke only of those things of which he was completely sure.

As the food was cleared from the table, Aresh stood up and bowed to the magistrate, 'Sir, you are a noble person, and though my father has sent me to be your assistant, I feel humbled already. I know very little, and hesitate to intrude; it's possible that in my ignorance I may do more harm than good.'

The magistrate said nothing for a while, nor did he ask Aresh to resume his seat. His wife also said nothing, and though she smiled at Aresh, it was with an intent that he couldn't quite fathom.

When the magistrate finally spoke it was in measured, thoughtful tones. 'Your father,' the magistrate said, 'sent you here. By questioning his decision you belittle his wisdom.'

Aresh bowed further at the reprimand.

'Nevertheless,' the magistrate added, 'it is good that you ask this question. A man must know his purpose, and be assured that he can fulfil it, otherwise he does nothing well. You may sit.'

When Aresh had settled himself again, the magistrate continued, 'What I need from you, Aresh, is what you have already displayed—an inquisitive mind and the courage to ask the questions your mind cannot answer. These though, are less important than the one most significant thing that I need from you, and that is compassion.

'I have grown old passing judgement on the follies and crimes of men and women, older by far than my real age. I have little patience or pity left in me.

Often, those that stand before me acting out their innocence are the same criminals that I have seen before, only with different faces and different names. Their crimes blur into each other, and perhaps I punish an innocent because I remember a guilty man who had stood in his place. I need your young eyes, and your young heart, to see and feel as I am no longer able to do.'

As Aresh made to speak, the magistrate raised a hand. 'You will learn from me also. You have come from a small community where people know each other, and some benefit of doubt can be accorded. Here, in Yasurat, there are only strangers. Blood and belonging don't hold, only law does. You will see me make seemingly harsh decisions, because kindness would be far crueller. That is what your father has sent you here to learn.'

And so Aresh began his career as the magistrate's assistant. Every day he would sit by the magistrate as judgements were passed, and every evening the magistrate would ask him about what he had seen and what he had learned. At first the magistrate would only correct him, but as the months rolled on,

Aresh would offer opinions and assert why he thought they were correct. They would argue late into the night over some small detail, but Aresh never knew if those arguments made any difference to the magistrate's decisions because those judgements would only ever be revealed in the courts.

Nobody came to petition Aresh, but his reputation grew in the city. Word went out onto the streets that the young man from the country, so beautiful and so serious with his power, spoke of people's lives and deaths and decided the fate of many. A woman came weeping to thank him once, the wife of a prisoner who had been released. Aresh didn't know how to respond, but denied any hand in the release.

As the months passed, the magistrate began taking Aresh to select, secluded gatherings where they would argue among people of power over what was to be done in a particular case, and whether it had merit and was deserving of mercy. It was at one such gathering that Aresh heard the rumours of war, and the name of Thakir. And then news came of battles with the nomads who roamed the steppes to the west and north. Among the circle of powerful men, Aresh saw maps and the shape of the world changing as little wooden armies were placed and replaced on the tables. He also heard of the bravery of a young captain who had earned a name for himself; a leader of men who rode at the right hand of the Amir of Thakir—Barab. Aresh was so full of his friend's glory that he blurted out, 'That's my brother.'

It was news of a sort. People knew little about Thakir, but now, in the time of war when heroes were made, Yasurat was interested in the story of these two young men who had grown up together and were now doing so well for themselves and the empire.

Powerful men asked Aresh about Thakir, about Barab, and about himself. Young women came to hear his stories. Even the magistrate's wife called him to her rooms occasionally, and, in the maze of silk and perfume, asked him to speak about friendship, youth and love.

In moments such as those Aresh longed for his friend, for the clarity he had known in Thakir. He envied Barab, fighting in battle, who knew friend from foe. He thought of his father, and wondered when his exile would end.

And then, one day, the magistrate's wife asked, 'Why do you hesitate?'

'My lady?'

'Why do you hesitate?' she asked again. 'Why do you tempt me constantly with your beauty that you know I desire?'

'My lady,' Aresh countered, 'what of your husband?'

The magistrate's wife smiled grimly, 'What of him? Does he deny himself beauty when he wants it? Why, then, should I?'

And Aresh bowed his head because he knew the magistrate was a powerful man, who denied himself little.

'Aresh,' she said again, and he trembled, for what young man, in the presence of a beautiful woman who speaks her desire, wouldn't tremble? And she laughed to see him so.

'No,' he said, and although it was an effort the word gave him strength. If only he had a friend in this city, if only he had his brother . . . 'No,' his refusal was firm. 'My Lady, your husband may allow himself many things, as may you. But that doesn't mean that I must be your tool.'

'As you wish,' she said, then tore a part of her gown and screamed. The guards rushed in, and news went out that the young man from Thakir was no more than a loathsome creature, who had assaulted the magistrate's wife, returning his master's kindness with such a heinous crime.

Aresh spent the next month alone in a small cell. Nobody visited him, and he heard nothing of the outside world. The guard who watched over him was surly, and wouldn't speak.

Then, one day his cell door opened and a figure entered, all cloaked in black. When the figure revealed his face, Aresh recognized the magistrate and kneeling before him, he said, 'Forgive me for the calumny I have brought upon your name.'

The magistrate laughed dryly. 'Don't bother to protect the reputation of the woman who put you here. I know what happened well enough.'

The magistrate's words filled Aresh with hope. Every youth believes in his own immortality. 'I'm to be released?'

The older man laughed again, a rough sound that echoed in the small cell. 'I see you have learned less from me than I have learned from you. No, Aresh, I can't declare your innocence, for that would mean admitting my wife's perfidy. And even though it may be true, it's not a truth I can declare. Too much rides upon her reputation, my reputation—I can't sacrifice all that for you.'

'Why are you here, then?' Aresh asked.

'To give you these,' the magistrate answered, giving him a leather bag. 'There is a letter from Thakir that came for you the day you were imprisoned, and the other is a gift from me.' He knocked on the door, and was let out.

Inside the bag Aresh found a dagger, a razor-edged one, and he knew that he could lure the guard into his cell and kill him. He would have to fight his way out, but he could escape from this prison. But to what end? He couldn't return to Thakir as a rapist and a murderer. His life would be that of a criminal, of a man who could never take his own name.

He turned his attention to the letter. Opening it, he immediately recognized the strong strokes of Barab's handwriting.

They tell me, my friend, that I'm a great fighter, a captain of men, the letter began, *but the truth is I am only a poor imitation of you. Every time I go into battle, every time I issue an order, or pass judgement, I think of what you would have done in my place. I am only a woodcutter's son; I don't know how to do these things. I hate the blood, the heat and the madness of killing—it makes no sense to me. Yet every time your father summons me, I obey. You have treated me as a brother, and I won't demean your name. But Aresh, I am close to breaking now. I vomit in the mornings before battle, and can't eat for a day after. Too often I have had to kill the terribly wounded men and animals that have been left on the battlefield. I can't bear their cries that echo in my mind day and night. I know that is what you would do; as an honourable man you wouldn't allow them to suffer so. But you're an Amir's son, and I'm only a poor copy. Tomorrow, I will flee and in a month's time I will be back at the place where we agreed to meet. It will be two years to the day when we made our promise. If you aren't there, my madness will destroy me.*

Aresh put down the letter. This is the day . . . the

day I promised to meet my brother. How could I have forgotten? How could I abandon him like this?

He examined the dagger carefully. It had a sharp edge, and after it broke the skin on the inside of his wrists, he felt it no more.

Barab sat by the road half a mile from Thakir. The day had been a long one; he had waited for his brother, but Aresh hadn't come. Unsure of what to do, Barab continued to linger. It was nearly midnight, and he was almost asleep when something brought him back to full wakefulness. He had heard no horse nor could he see one, but Aresh was there.

'Brother,' Barab said, 'I had given up hope.'

Aresh smiled.

Nobody said a word after the Begum finished her story. Food and drink had been set out before them, but few had touched what was on offer. It was only at the end that one of the servants brought a small dish, full of small slivers of roasted meat for the Begum. She raised an eyebrow, and the servant bowed his head. 'From your hunt,' he said.

The storyteller watched the Begum raise one of the morsels to her exquisite mouth before he addressed Mehrunnisa, 'May I be so bold as to mention that I have another tale?'

The maid looked to the Begum, who nodded almost imperceptibly.

Mehrunnisa turned back to the storyteller, 'But not for today.'

The storyteller nodded, and then smiled shyly as he bowed his head. 'Perhaps I could stay another day?'

The Begum nodded, and Mehrunnisa said, 'It is permitted.'

THE SOLDIER

It was a difficult night. The wind was turning cold as autumn drew near. The storyteller heard it howling its loneliness outside the haveli, and it kept him awake far beyond the time when exhaustion should have sent him to sleep.

At some point of the night he rose on an impulse and left his room. He made his way along the dimly lit corridors and stopped just ahead of the last turn before the outer gates. He knew there would be guards there, and he would be unable to explain exactly what he was doing, and why it had become so necessary for him to go outside and listen to what the wind was saying.

Instead he leaned against the wall, letting the

cold seep into him, heating the house in his own small way. The chill that settled in his bones comforted him, calmed him somewhat. They were old companions—enemies if not friends—the cold, the wind and he. It was impossible to imagine a life without them. And he needed them now more than ever, needed them to bind him, to trap his passion so that it didn't run amok and embarrass him. He had learnt long ago to find comfort in the familiarity of his discomforts; he would have been lost without them.

The Begum's story, her challenge, had taken him by surprise. It had been so very long since somebody had matched him, and, truth be told, outstripped him. He had become complacent in his mastery, jaded in the confidence of his own excellence. He had thought to lay down a challenge among his enemies, show these savages, who had never known the glory of Delhi, of Shahjahanabad, what civilization meant. He had anticipated insults, maybe even some violence if their words had failed them. But he hadn't imagined being bested. What a shocking joy it was to be defeated, to be in love again.

How long had it been since he had burned like this, with the fervour to prove himself, to win the approval of a beautiful woman, to change the shape of her lips by the power of a story that he had to tell?

The Begum's beauty had been only one of the things that drew him to her, though far from unimportant. Being the man that he was, with nothing to have and hold, with a life lived around the edges, he had always considered himself the most liberated of men. Since he wanted nothing from the world, he felt he had the right to praise or condemn it freely.

It was an argument that might have been impressive if he didn't fall in love with every beautiful thing he saw. Even if he didn't seek to possess the things he desired, his longing left him involved, even implicated, with the world.

The storyteller, however, always pretended otherwise. He would use any excuse to disguise his reaction to beauty. It was probably why he had responded the way he had to the Begum, by telling her a story about the impossibility of love. Her response had freed him from the fear of being rejected, but it had also trapped him. Whereas earlier all he had wanted to do was to preach about the impossibility of things, now he wanted to be able to earn her respect.

Words from a long time ago echoed in his thoughts, 'You're never really prepared to listen unless you're prepared to change.' He must have heard that at one of those gatherings of Sufi poets that he had attended in his youth, when he was still consumed with the fever of his first, his greatest, passion. He had thought about it over the years, but he had never been convinced of the full truth of it. There was something there, yes, but he couldn't be sure whether it was as straightforward as it seemed. Thinking about it now, he still wasn't sure, but it gave him the key that he needed.

The only way to answer the Begum was to retell her story, as well as his own. It would be a sign that he had listened, and changed; and a test to see if she could accept the changes that he would make in her story, in her world.

The knowledge gave him peace. He didn't know what story he would tell in the morning, but he knew the how and the why of it. He would find a way.

With that thought in mind, he made his way back to his room.

It was the sun that woke him, the warmth reaching inside his blanket and uncurling him like a leaf welcoming the dawn. It had been many years since the sun had awakened him. In Delhi, it had always been far away, the light being filtered by all the great houses before it reached his humble one.

He heard the clatter of utensils and the sizzle of hot oil and guessed that he was somewhere near the kitchens. This newfound awareness brought on an almost crushing hunger, but the storyteller stayed his ground. He was a guest in this house, and he would have to wait until he was summoned. He recalled his little house in Shahjahanabad then. There had been nothing there, really, nothing to show for his fame and the respect of his name. He had had no wife, no lover, no family to go home to. There had only been his two servants, the old man and his wife, who had looked after his meagre needs. In fact it had been more theirs than his, and after the raiders had destroyed it, the desolation had been greater for them than for him.

He had paid them the little he could, before he had had his own small store of goods sent to Awadh, where an admirer had said a place would be made available. Maybe they would follow him in time, but for now he had nothing, and was compelled to survive on charity. Even on the generosity of his enemies. He thought about that, about the story that the Begum had told, and realized that she had left a door open for him in the story.

He was so lost in thought that he did not see Afzal enter, and it was only the sound of the tray being set down by shaky hands that brought the storyteller back to the present.

'The Begum has asked you to make yourself available in two hours' time,' Afzal said.

The storyteller nodded, and then Afzal asked, 'It is questioned whether our guest has many changes of clothing. The guard who carried your luggage remarked on how light the load was.'

A flush crept up the storyteller's neck. He had retained only a few sets of clothes with him to see him through the journey to Lucknow.

'It is enough,' he replied.

The old man nodded, and said, 'It is the custom

of the Mirza household that a certain form of dress be maintained. In honour of her husband's wishes, the Begum has asked for some clothes to be sent to you. It is hoped that you will do us the honour.'

The storyteller nodded, 'The honour shall be mine.'

A couple of hours later, bathed and fed, and dressed like a minor noble, the storyteller found himself being led out to the grounds. A shamiana had been set up and within its billowing cloth walls, rugs and gautakias were placed. It was here that the storyteller found the Begum enjoying the soft strains of a sarod, while she sat surrounded by her retinue.

'The Begum hopes that you spent a peaceful night,' Mehrunnisa spoke as he entered.

'I am rested, and I have a story to tell,' was all he replied. The look that the Begum gave him upon hearing his answer made him wonder whether she knew he had gone wandering through the corridors the night before.

The maid nodded. 'You will permit the sarod player to come to the end of his piece.'

Some people are born to violence (the storyteller began as the sarod player finished). It isn't a habit they acquire, or a lesson they learn, but an innate part of themselves, something natural and true that makes them whole. However, no one is born fully aware of his self; it is often the parents, either of blood or choice, who show the way. Like birds that push their hatchlings out of the nest, some human parents, too, fling their children out into the void. And once the children have learnt the use of their wings, walking is never enough.

Barab had two fathers; one who showed him how to fly, and another who forced him to. A woodcutter's son, he grew up pretending to be the brother of the Amir's son. And though he had already been named once, it was the Amir who gave him his official name. But sometimes, by mistake, or simply because love can never be completely commanded, his mother whispered the other name, the name he could no longer claim—'Taka'.

It was like living with a ghost in the house, a presence that could be sensed, but never seen. Barab grew up haunted by this name that his mother would speak, but never acknowledge. The oddest thing was how his body would react, how he would turn to the calling of that name without understanding why, sometimes even despite knowing that he shouldn't, only to see his mother turning away.

Sometimes, at night, words would come out of him; at other times it was just grunts and uncertain noise. Sometimes he would be contorted with laughter, or tears would flow down his face. Aresh, his brother in all but name, would be frightened, and ask what was happening.

Only then would Barab find his voice. Everything else would be lost—his body, his emotions—everything but his voice. 'Shhhh, it's Taka.'

And so Aresh learnt about the ghost too, learnt to fear him, and knew that his name must never be spoken. He also learned that his brother was strong, that although Barab was haunted by this demon that rose in the darkness, it couldn't totally possess him. Aresh knew Barab would keep him safe. He was too young to understand that maybe it was only his presence, only his voice in the dark, that allowed Barab to reclaim his self and kept Taka at bay.

As they grew older Taka made fewer appearances and gradually, Aresh forgot about him, as children do. But Barab never did; he had grown stronger over time, knowing that Taka lurked like a fever in his blood, and a moment's weakness was all he needed to claim Barab. And even then he was taken off guard when Taka finally emerged.

It began with a knife, or actually two. His father, the woodcutter, had made them for the boys as a gift when they turned eleven and were considered 'men'. Barab reached for his, but it was Taka who grasped the knife and drew it wonderingly in the air, watching the sunlight gleam off the edge. It was Taka who flexed the muscles in his arm, who bared his teeth in pleasure as the knife glided easily in the air, cutting edge up, point out, held straight by the thumb that guided each and every flicker. It was Taka who felt the throb of violence in the wood, and who instinctively knew that the steel of the blade would taste like blood. It was Taka who laughed in the woods, in sudden delight; Taka who finally took possession of Barab, held his body and laughed with his voice.

It was Taka his father saw.

In fear, wonderingly, the woodcutter heard himself ask, 'Boys, do you know the story of Taka and Wara?'

The name hit Barab like cold water to the face, and he struggled to reclaim his body, to speak. Aresh only shook his head.

Slowly, eyes fixed on Barab, the woodcutter started telling the story. The words strengthened his voice, and in the sunlit woods he told the story of the wolf cub named Taka, who was adopted by a young mother and raised alongside her human child. He told them how the wolf grew up and one day saved his human brother from a group of wild dogs, only to be killed by the same woman who had reared him because she could only see him as a wolf when the love had dimmed from her eyes.

Aresh wept at the ending of the story, 'That was a bitter tale! Why did the poor wolf have to die? Just because the woman stopped loving him? Why couldn't she just let him loose? What kind of love is that?'

Barab disagreed. 'It was a good end,' he said, his voice rough with the effort of fighting, and winning against, Taka within him.

Aresh turned to him in surprise, as much because of the weariness in Barab's voice as by what he said.

But it was the woodcutter who asked, 'Why do you say that?'

'Death and honour,' Barab murmured, and then, 'in that death there was honour.' He explained after a moment, 'Taka was a wolf. He could not have lived his life being a brother to a human. At some point of time he would have embraced his true nature, or worse, the love would have dimmed in his brother's eyes just as it had in his mother's. Who knows what would have happened then? This was a better end. Taka repaid his debt; he proved his love while it still existed. He died guiltless, without betraying those whom he had loved.'

It was a long speech. Usually it was Aresh who would speak for them, but this time he was too stunned to respond.

'It was a good end,' Barab repeated, and wept.

By the time they returned to the woodcutter's cottage, Barab was burning with fever. For three nights and two days it consumed him as he rambled in his delirium, sweating and thrashing about. And through this time he never let go of the knife, holding it firmly. But even in his blind, insensate state he hurt nobody with the knife, cutting neither himself nor those who took care of him.

When Barab awoke on the third day, finally himself, he saw Aresh asleep in a cot next to him. He tried to get up without waking Aresh, but his bed creaked with his shifting weight. Aresh got up instantly, moving from deep sleep to full consciousness as if he had been napping for only a moment. It had always made Barab wonder, and he had envied Aresh this ability, but right now he was just glad to see his brother next to him.

Barab tried to speak, but his throat was dry, and the words wouldn't come. So he smiled.

'At last, you lazy ass,' Aresh said.

'How long?' Barab rasped.

When Aresh told him, Barab shook his head in disbelief. Then he saw the knife clutched in his hand and his smile died.

His hand was so cramped that he could barely move his fingers. The slightest movement brought tears to his eyes. It took a long time, but Aresh didn't say a word until it was over. He offered neither help nor comment as Barab removed the knife from himself and then slowly, gently, started to massage the palm of his hand.

It was only then that Aresh spoke. 'I had this made,' he said, pulling out a wide leather belt with a sheath.

Barab looked at it for a long moment, still massaging his hand, and then smiled slowly, 'Tell me that you didn't get one for yourself.'

Aresh grinned, and pointed to the leather belt hanging from a peg on the wall. It was an exact replica of the one he held.

'Style is everything,' Aresh declared in solemn tones, and grinned like a fool.

Barab was unsure which of them started laughing first, but they were both guffawing when his mother looked in, relieved to find her son had recovered from the sudden fever.

In the days that followed though, it became clear that something fundamental had changed in Barab. He recovered the weight that he had lost during the fever and gained muscle—the width of his shoulders and depth of his chest making him look shorter than he was. It was only his face that remained lean and hungry, something in it that he couldn't hide.

He had always been a late-riser, but now he slept late at night and woke up before dawn to go wandering, sometimes running, through the forest for the sheer thrill of it. His body, his muscles, demanded strengthening, even punishment. A part of him knew that he was suppressing Taka within himself, but he also knew that this hunger was for violence, for war. He would practise with the soldiers now, fighting with wooden swords. Aresh practised as well, and had talent, but when it came to Barab the soldiers truly competed.

There were times when he would lose himself in the grace of it; the clean movement of the blade, the balance of his body, and the pure power of the right move made at the right moment—it would all come together in his head, in his heart. He fought like a hawk flew—because it was in his nature, because it was his reality. And then there were times when he would stumble, when a chance blow would cause real pain. Those were the times when he couldn't find the right place within himself, and a dark spark was enough for him to lose control. He had no name for the feeling; it began with anger, but became something else so quickly that it belied definition.

The end would always be the same. He would be left sweating, every muscle in his body thrumming like the string of a mandolin, standing over a defeated opponent. And he would realize that he had lost again; that all the discipline and strength he had gained couldn't keep the animal locked inside forever. He was only strengthening the jaws of the wolf.

Then, one day, an entourage came from Yasurat, the capital of the empire. Among them was a young girl, about the same age as Barab and Aresh. Both boys saw that she was pretty, but it was Aresh who was overcome by her beauty. Glancing around him at all the other young men awestruck by the girl's grace, Barab realized that it was only he who was unaffected.

It was amusing, and odd. And since these things had a deeper meaning for him than others, a dark mood engulfed Barab. Aresh had started dressing in his most presentable clothes, and looking at them now, Barab said suddenly, 'We can't be friends.'

Aresh, caught off guard, was hurt, and asked, 'Why do you say that?'

Seeing the hurt on Aresh's face, Barab found that he couldn't tell the truth, so he said, 'Look at us, Aresh. You are the Amir's only son and my father is a humble woodcutter. You will have your wealth, your fine clothes and your power. I will always struggle to keep up with you, and I will always fail.'

Aresh thought about what the other boy had said, and then grinned, 'This is about that girl, isn't it? The one who is visiting the castle with her family?'

It was such a ridiculous thing to say and yet so close to the truth, that Barab blushed. Aresh hooted with laughter, 'Oooh! Barab is in love!'

'Shut up!' Barab grumbled and took a swipe at Aresh.

But Aresh was enjoying himself far too much to stop. 'Barab is in love with Little-Princess-I-Am-Very-Fine!' he teased. Barab tried to catch him, but the other boy evaded his grasp. In the end Barab gave up, and grumpily sat down to pluck at the grass.

'Why don't you sneak into her room?' Aresh suggested from a safe distance. 'Then you can declare your love for her?'

It was then that Barab realized how truly Aresh had been named for he was as generous as his name would have him be. Barab knew that Aresh was smitten with the girl, but here he was offering to help his brother court her. He realized something else too: in their banter he was simply Barab, there was no Taka there, no lust for violence, no animal breath in his own mouth.

So he nodded assent, and tried to court the girl because Aresh had been generous, and Barab wouldn't disappoint the one friend he had, who kept him human. They failed. Barab had a nagging feeling that the girl knew he wasn't really interested, but it was all right.

The nonchalance of adolescence does not last forever, and it was the Amir who ended things. He summoned the two young men and told Aresh that he would leave for Yasurat, and then turning to Barab, he said, 'Were you brothers in blood your paths would still diverge one day—the elder son rules and the younger protects, that is how our world works. When Aresh leaves, you will join the army that defends these borders.'

The Amir had heard about Barab, about how the soldiers, who had once taught him out of idleness and good nature, now fought to keep up with the young man. He had gone to the training arena and seen the way that the other soldiers parted way for Barab. Seeing Aresh sitting on the sidelines while the men battled, the Amir was both pleased and dismayed. It was good that Barab had become the fighter that he was. It would help Aresh to have a companion who commanded such respect among the army, here, along the border near the savages. But it could be a disadvantage too if Aresh were overshadowed, as he could easily be, as he seemed content to be, by the woodcutter's son.

So the Amir passed his judgement, and didn't know that he was destroying Barab's world.

As Aresh rode away from the city, Barab accompanied him, and wondered if he should have told his brother the truth that time, long ago. Should he have said, 'No, brother, it isn't love, it is madness that runs through my blood,' when the young girl had come from Yasurat. It was too late now. There wasn't enough time to set things straight, and even if the truth did come out, what would it prove? The Amir had set the course of their lives; nothing Barab said would change that now. The desperation grew in him, and though it was unmanly to do so, Barab wept and asked, 'Tell me, should I say farewell?'

Aresh gripped his friend's hand in a strong clasp, and replied, 'Barab, you've been truer to me than most brothers are.'

In that reply Barab saw hope, and thought that if he could only hold for a while, until Aresh returned, he could keep his humanity, his sanity from slipping away. 'Promise me, then,' he demanded, 'that two years from now we will meet again at this place.'

'I promise,' Aresh vowed, and they parted.

From that day on Barab lived for that promise, but outwardly other things happened. At first there was little change in his life. He had spent so much time among the soldiers that joining the army only meant that he slept in the barracks now, and woke early with the other young men. The Amir wasn't a person who would waste talent, and now that the threat to Aresh had been removed, he was content to build Barab into a captain of men.

Every evening the Amir and Barab sat down and played a complex game of strategy on a wooden table, with armies, castles and siege engines being moved into place as they fought bygone battles, and wars the world hadn't yet seen.

At first Barab was clumsy and confused.

'This is dishonest,' he said one day, out of frustration.

'What do you mean?' the Amir asked.

Barab held up one of the carved pieces meant to depict a soldier with a sword, 'No two soldiers are equal. It isn't just placement and reach that determines the outcome of a battle, but will and determination.'

The Amir nodded. 'Yes, that's true, but it isn't the pieces that will show their will, it is you.'

'I don't understand,' Barab said.

'You're making the mistake of all beginners,' the Amir explained. 'Think of how a man leads people. It isn't because he tells them to go in one direction or the other. No captain has the time to order things clearly in battle. No. A good captain wields his men just as if they were a sword held in his hand, by his will, because they are just an extension of himself.'

The Amir picked up a piece and holding it, he continued, 'Barab, a soldier, a piece, knows nothing and can only control himself, but a captain knows everything, feels everything that goes on in battle. If you look at this battle board as only a place where you can move pieces here and there, you'll always lose. But if you choose to look at them as expressions of your will, of your will set against mine, then you have a chance.'

Barab still didn't understand. That wasn't how he looked at things, and one day, in a fit of blind fury, of the type he sometimes experienced when he lost control, he attacked the Amir's carefully assembled pieces with his lowest soldiers, scattering the board, and making the Amir defend, defend, defend, until the bitter end when Barab's pieces were mostly gone, and the Amir claimed the board.

'Yes,' the Amir smiled, 'that is how you fight.'

Barab, who had been exhilarated in putting up the fight, understood then that it was his madness the Amir wanted, nothing else. He could accept it. It was only carved wooden soldiers on a board; and he learnt when to give in to the madness in his heart, and like the practice sword fights he wasn't sure if he was strengthening himself, or the wolf within him.

A year passed like that, and then a few months more, while the Amir slowly taught Barab the meaning of war, and despite the grumbling of some of his senior commanders, gave him more and more responsibility. With winter, the games and the practise came to an end. It was the coldest year that the people in Thakir could recall. As it progressed, leopards and wolves, starved of their natural prey, broke cover from the forests to hunt livestock.

The Amir readied his men; he knew the wild animals wouldn't be the only ones hungry in the hills. It was a long border, and when the raiders came on their swift ponies to attack a small village, they caught the people by surprise. The news reached Thakir half a day later when an exhausted man on a half-dead horse came to tell the Amir. The soldiers set off in pursuit almost immediately.

By the time they reached the village, it had been torched. There was nothing living in the whole hamlet; bodies littered the street, blackened and mutilated.

'This is too bloody,' the Amir said. Then suddenly he turned his horse, and said, 'We must ride fast. Thakir is under attack.'

They were almost too late, but smug in their belief that the Amir and his men would go off to chase the perpetrators of the massacre, the raiders had miscalculated and took too long to follow up with their attack on Thakir. Nobody had attacked the city in living memory. Its markets and houses had spilled over the boundaries within which they could be easily defended. The sheer audacity of the raiders might have led to success, but once the Amir was back they had no chance.

Stationing teams of horsemen at the three access routes to the city, the Amir let the raiders ride on into the city where they found only barricaded houses and the army ready to welcome them. Their escape routes were cut off by the horsemen that rode in behind them. The butchery was horrendous. Not even one raider escaped alive. Everybody had heard the story of the massacre by then, and there was no forgiveness for these wolves.

At the end of it the Amir said, 'This is just the

beginning. They would have never attacked the city if it was for just one raid.'

The people accepted his words without question. He had been right too many times before, including about Barab. Older captains had complained about giving the young man such authority before he had even proved himself, but Barab had been a killer like no other.

The Amir was praised at the end of it, and Barab, too, was given his due share of respect, even if it was born out of fear. People had seen him ride through the streets wielding a large battleaxe black with blood. His soldiers had seen him kill and take pleasure in it. But what had impressed them was the way Barab had controlled his men completely, moving them where they were most needed, withdrawing and relaxing them when he had a chance. Not one of the soldiers under his command had died, although they had their fair share of wounds. He seemed to have been made for war, and his men were ready to follow him till the ends of the earth.

Barab said nothing, made no comment that showed he had noticed the change around him, but he stopped smiling except when he was making small talk with his men. He saw to the wounded, making sure that those who were severely injured received proper care, and were sent to their homes. When one of them complained, Barab said, 'You heard the Amir. This is only the beginning. You'll recover in time to see more battles. I'd rather you be strong for them than throw away your life now when you are weak.'

The Amir had started to plan, taking down old, detailed maps of the cold steppes to the west and north from where the raiders had come. The first ruse had failed, but it had still meant a village had burned and all of its inhabitants butchered. The Amir had no intention of waiting for a repeat performance. He would take the battle into the raiders' own lands.

The first attack had been audacious, but it had been almost flirtatious in its lightness. The next few attacks were major battles, skirmishes involving hundreds of men. The Amir had sent out scouts to watch the nearest streams and waterholes, and advance warning helped the people of Thakir to anticipate and plan their strategy. The Amir's men had gone to all the major villages, recruiting people for the army, sometimes even employing force. They needed all the men that they could gather.

It was a long border war, with battles sometimes fought back to back over a period of a few weeks. The soldiers were soon exhausted, and rested recruits replaced the seasoned hands. At the head of the army was the Amir, and he stayed on the field. At his right hand was Barab, who became darker and fiercer by the day. As his hair lengthened and his gaunt features took on a harder edge, the men started calling him the Wolf of Thakir.

It was an indication of how lost he was in himself that Barab only heard the name he had been given when the spring came, and the attacks were slackening off. That was when things started to go bad for him. Coming back to the city, he couldn't handle the silence, the peace. He spent long days riding in the hills around the city, searching for enemies that were no longer there. He'd been sickened during the war, but only because he had enjoyed it so much, and he didn't know what that made him. He didn't know how he'd face Aresh when his brother returned in a few months' time.

Barab went back to the hut he shared with his woodcutter father, and spent the days in silent hard work. Then, one day, as he was splitting wood, the axe in his hand went wild, and he couldn't stop himself. He needed to do something with it, he needed to kill. Frozen, he stood with the axe half-raised until the first human walked in front of his vision. Raising the axe for a killing blow, he heard his mother say, 'Taka, no!'

His vision cleared, and dropping the axe before him, he ran into the forest, ran until he was completely exhausted, until every muscle in his body ached and he could have harmed nobody and nothing. Only then did he allow himself to stop, to rest, to weep, leaning against a tree high in the hills.

He was lost now, and he knew it.

The next day he went straight to the army camp, and found a messenger waiting from the Amir for him. He knew it was to do with the border war, and he was immediately ready. The hunger rose again, to command, to control and to kill. He should have been sickened by it, but couldn't be.

'I have received reports of one large, last sortie,' the Amir said. 'It seems that the raiders have brought together all that remains of their scattered men for a large assault. Our men are exhausted, and most have returned to their homes. There isn't time to prepare to meet them. Their army needs to be delayed.'

Barab nodded. It took him only a moment to consider the options. 'I'll need three dozen men,' he said.

'They have at least two thousand,' the Amir said.

'I'll only be delaying them,' Barab answered.

Something in his face must have given him away, because the Amir, a man who shied away from physical touch, reached out across the table to grasp Barab's shoulder. The men said nothing to each other, and after a moment Barab got up. As he was about to leave, he said, 'I'd like to write a letter to Aresh, do you think it could be delivered?'

'Of course,' the Amir said.

So Barab, who realized now that he would never see Aresh in the flesh again, sat down to write his brother a letter. He thought about writing the truth, and then changed his mind. Instead he conjured up in his mind the boy he used to be before he knew violence, before he learnt about his other name, before he became the Wolf of Thakir. For a moment he became that innocent child again, and was crippled with shame and horror at the war.

It was that Barab that wrote a letter to Aresh. *They tell me, my friend, that I'm a great fighter, a captain of men, but the truth is I am but a poor imitation of you. Every time I go into battle, every time I issue an order, or pass judgement, I think of what you would have done in my place. I am only a woodcutter's son; I don't know how to do these things. I hate the blood, the heat and the madness of killing—it makes no sense to me. Yet every time your father summons me, I obey. You have treated me as a brother, and I won't demean your name. But Aresh, I am close to breaking now. I vomit in the mornings before battle, and can't eat for a day after. Too often I have had to kill the terribly wounded men and animals that have been left on the battlefield. I can't bear their cries that echo in my mind day and night. I know that is what you would do; as an honourable man you wouldn't allow them to suffer so. But you're an Amir's son, and I'm only a poor copy. Tomorrow, I will flee and in a month's time I will be back at the place where we agreed to meet. It will be two years to the day when we made our promise. If you aren't there, my madness will destroy me.*

After sealing the letter, the Wolf of Thakir left along with his three dozen men. They all knew the nature of the battle, and each said to the other, 'Death and honour. Death and honour.' All except one, who was to act as the watcher, and report back to the Amir.

They say that Barab caught sight of the raiders just when he was about to eat some grapes. Flinging them aside, he said, 'Why wait?' and charged at his enemies. Over the course of the week his men continued to attack the raiders' army during day and night, at the most unexpected of times.

They continued to be killed, but the raiders were delayed. They had to be perpetually on alert. At every watering hole they had to deal with traps, with poison. Unexpected holes appeared under their feet, sudden spikes claimed lives, and fires at night scared their horses. The Wolf of Thakir directed the defence of the city from beyond the grave.

It gave the Amir time to prepare, and by the time the raiders reached the city, the Amir had his men ready. The raiders broke at the first charge, nervous and disheartened by the perpetual raids on their camp over the last week from the men who charged to their deaths, two or three at a time, attacking an army of thousands.

They say, also, that the ghost of Barab, the Wolf of Thakir, was seen riding out of the city to a forest glade, where he waited and waited until he was met by another ghost, that of Aresh.

There was silence when the story came to an end, or perhaps it was a set of silences, since the reactions of the audience had many flavours.

It was one of the guards who spoke first. 'It seems you have little love for raiders, for the captains that rise from outside fortified walls to shake the arrogant in their heedless debauchery.'

The storyteller blinked, but he had never bowed his head before anyone, certainly not before some ignorant guard just one step removed from the savages he guarded against. 'I have little love for the destroyers of civilization, even less for those that don't understand what they destroy, like heedless children full only of their capability at destruction, maggots that feel they have conquered a tiger simply because they feed on its decaying corpse.'

Before the guard could move, the Begum had raised a hand. 'There is a tradition in this house regarding guests.'

Then she turned to look at the storyteller, speaking to him directly for the first time, 'And there is a tradition also regarding those who insult the Mirza.'

Her voice was cold with those words, colder than the wind had been last night, and the storyteller realized just what he had done. He wanted to cry out, to say that he had only wished to speak a common language, to become a part of the story she had told. What did he care about cities and raiders, what did he care that the master of the haveli was a brigand, but of a greater sort, so that he was called a captain of men, a Mirza?

But then that would have been a lie.

And isn't that the tragedy of love, it's utter and complete deceit, that you can only be true in it, that you only wish to reveal your full truth to the one you love, with no frills and no lies, that you want to be loved as you are? That you wish to be loved for your truth, and not your ability to hide it? What was it that Mirza Jaan-e-Jaan had written? *Yeh dil kab ishq ke qabil raha hai/ Kahaan isko dimagh-o-dil raha hai*? When has this heart been capable of loving?/ When has it had the intelligence [to play the game] of love, this heart of mine?

The storyteller had spoken his truth, from the heart, and not from a mind bent on playing the game of love, and his truth was that he hated the raiders who fed off the remains of his city. He despised them, and knew that they were destroying something that they couldn't build, and whose greatness they couldn't even fully grasp. Oh, there had been other cities before Delhi, there would be others after it. Now that the Mughals had faded into petty parasites themselves, some new tribe would arise, maybe from the north, maybe from the west, maybe from the south, maybe even from here, in Rohillakhand. But it would be a long while before they even knew what they had lost, much less before they could try and replicate the greatness that they were destroying.

He had spoken his truth, that he was their enemy. How could he expect love now, though it was his love that had made him say what he had? Isn't that love, the sum of all love, that you give no thought to safety, and walk into its house without question, when only caution might have saved you? But all you want to do is serve, so you betray yourself.

'The story was of a place long away, of a time far past. It was not this guest's intention to show any disrespect, especially not to the Mirza, whose salt he has now eaten, and whose hospitality dresses him in the little honour that he has.'

The moment held, until Mehrunnisa asked, 'Yesterday my Begum had asked you two questions. Where will you go from here, and when will you be off?'

The storyteller saw the slight twitch that was the Begum's only reaction, but the words had already been said, and in her name. The Begum nodded.

'Your Begum may be pleased to know that I leave

for the court of the Nawab of Awadh, and as soon as I am capable of it.'

'It is not the custom of this house that a guest leaves in the middle of the day, only enemies do that,' the Begum said, and the storyteller bowed.

'We shall not detain you if you wish to leave immediately, but it was our thought that you would attend to us in the evening, and we would pay you back for your story with one last one of our own.'

The storyteller bowed even lower.

'In that case our guest shall leave tomorrow morning,' the Begum declared.

THE MAGISTRATE'S WIFE AND THE GIRL

The story had been so unexpected. It was as if somebody had taken her own words and shown them to be only a part of a realization. She felt like a child again, when her father had sat her down and shown her what things meant exactly, how a slingshot worked, how to hold a bow.

The storyteller had taken her own fable, a story of her own lands and opened vistas within it that she had not seen, had undressed her like a lover, with care, marvelling at a beauty that she had never noticed.

And then the guard had spoken, and the moment shattered before her. She had tried to intervene and save it, to save the storyteller, and this love that had sprung up so unexpectedly in her life. But then Mehrunnisa had used the Begum's own words, and she realized how impossible it had all become, so quickly, so irrevocably. All she could do now was hold on to his company for the evening, and keep him safe for the time being.

And isn't that love, the sum of all love, that you are so stunned by it that you can't stretch your hand out to grasp it, even as it slips away?

But she couldn't let him go that easily. She wanted to show him her estates, to prove and explain that they were more than raiders here in Rohillakhand. So she requested him to accompany her, and saw in his eyes the heartbreak that he was trying to hide as he assented.

She couldn't stand the hurt in his glance and moved instead to the stables, where they mounted their steeds. Once astride, she was in command. This was familiar territory, and the wielding of power came easily to her. She showed him the mango orchards and the grove of guava trees; she called the peasant children and distributed a small bounty in coins, more than their parents earned in a week.

With each passing moment she saw the storyteller ease into his saddle. He would never make a great horseman, but as he lost himself in her directions, in the works of the estate, he seemed to become more comfortable, accepting his place and his fate. When she thought it was safe to speak, she told a story, the last thing she could give him, even though she spoke to the air in front of her for she could not address him directly.

Popularity is a fickle thing. Aresh would have been surprised by the fame that came to him after his death. But they say that ghosts are deaf, and it is doubtful if his spirit heard, or would have cared.

In the days after his death, Aresh came to symbolize the sacrifices that the people of Thakir had made for the empire. News had arrived, carried by swift messengers, describing how Thakir had defeated the greatest invasion in living memory. The messages described how the young and the brave had thrown away their lives to keep the marauders at bay. The name of one man, Barab, the Wolf of Thakir, was praised above that of all others, and his death was mourned greatly. And Barab had grown up as a brother to Aresh, whom Yasurat, the capital of a careless empire, had murdered.

All across the city people heard about the battles in far off Thakir, and were caught up in the romance of it. Lost in the ennui of daily life, they praised this man who had shown that people could still be heroes if they dared. But underneath their praise, they were ashamed of themselves, of the smallness of their lives, and they knew that they were incapable of such heroism. So they searched for somebody they could look down upon.

Thus it came to pass that even as Aresh was laid on blocks of ice, dressed in purest white for the three days of mourning, voices were raised condemning the magistrate's wife. The next day, the voices rose again until, by the evening, even friends of the magistrate's wife condemned her.

It was then that she broke her silence and sent messengers to the most notable women of the city, inviting them to the temple on the third and last day of mourning. And despite their censure, those she had invited came to the temple, maybe out of friendship, or maybe out of fear, or just curiosity.

The magistrate's wife met them in the outer hall, and said, 'Sisters, even in the temple I hear the story they tell. They say I tried to seduce this young man by beauty, and then by threats. And when he refused, I had him imprisoned, and in his shame, he killed himself.'

There were murmurs at this because it wasn't the practice to speak of such things so bluntly. The magistrate's wife didn't heed the voices; instead she added, 'I don't know why he killed himself, but it is true that I enticed him, and when he refused me, I condemned him by my lies.'

Soft cries of 'Shame' echoed in the hall, growing louder until one of the women stepped forward, and declared, 'Sister, if you have called us here to confess your crime, then you do so in an unseemly manner. Your eyes should be lowered by the weight of your sins and your voice should carry the guilt you feel. Instead you are proud, and admit your crime almost like delivering a challenge.'

'Sin? Guilt? Crime?' the magistrate's wife asked. 'How can you know of these things? How can you judge my actions, until you see what injustice was visited upon me?'

'Injustice? What injustice?' many voices demanded.

For a moment the magistrate's wife was silent, and then in a soft voice—lonely and hurt as that of a small child—she questioned them, 'Have you seen him?' And then again, eagerly, 'Have you seen him?'

All but one head shook in denial, but the magistrate's wife did not notice the one that didn't. 'Then how can you *know*?' she wailed.

There was such power, such appeal, in her voice that the other women were caught unprepared.

'You must see him,' she declared then, even though custom dictated that only family looked upon a dead man's face while he lay in the temple. 'But before you do, I must ask you to do one thing.'

'What is that, sister?' all but one asked, caught by this mystery and the possibility of a revelation.

The magistrate's wife gestured, and a maid came to her side, carrying a basket full of sharp knives, their edges glinting wickedly in the wavering torchlight.

'Each of you must hold a knife by the blade as you look upon him. Only then will you know what has been done to me.'

It was a strange request, but the hall was brimming over with curiosity and when one woman walked up to grasp a knife by the blade, the others followed. Gripping their knives firmly, they made their way into the inner temple to look upon Aresh, and to each of them the same thing happened.

They had heard that Aresh was a beautiful man, and had dismissed the praise—isn't all youth beautiful? And isn't all such beauty ephemeral, a thing of the moment, not to be remarked on by the wise who knew better? Yet when their eyes fell upon Aresh all such thoughts fled them because he was lovely beyond words, so beautiful that the word itself lost its meaning.

Each woman gasped. Each unconsciously clenched her hands. And each hissed in pain when the sharp edge of the knife bit into her flesh and drew blood.

Only the magistrate's wife sighed.

'Do you see?' she asked in a voice tinged with both victory and defeat. 'Do you see what was done to me?'

For a while nobody answered, and the only sound was that of fire crackling in the bracket lamps on the walls.

Then one of the women, the oldest and richest among them, walked up to the magistrate's wife and touched her on the arm. It wasn't a gesture of forgiveness but there was understanding there, and something else. As the women left, silent and awed, the magistrate's wife knew that each of them was relieved that Aresh hadn't come to stay at their house, and each of them was jealous that he had not.

In the end only one woman remained, but the magistrate's wife didn't recognize her. She was younger than Aresh who lay, coldly beautiful, between them.

'My name is Nisia,' the young woman said at last. 'I knew him before.' She smiled bitterly. 'He wasn't so beautiful then,' she said, and raised her hand. 'See, I have cut myself, too.'

The magistrate's wife could feel resentment and envy overwhelm her. She had faced all her pain, had taken the bitterest part of what Fate had to offer, and bit down on it. But this news managed to surprise her. Isn't that the brutal truth of love, that you can never choose the ache it leaves you with, that it doesn't matter if you offer to take the pain on your unprotected breast, it will still stab you in the back? She had no defences left anymore, and began to weep gently.

Nisia made no gesture, said not a word until the magistrate's wife recovered her composure enough to command, 'Speak. Tell me your tragedy.'

Nisia ignored the spite and sarcasm in those words; she didn't have the energy to contend with them anymore.

'I don't know if it *is* my tragedy. I don't even know if it's a story complete in itself. You see, the story was his,' she pointed to Aresh, 'and I don't know if I was ever truly a part of it, or if it's only my vanity that makes me believe so.

'As a child I believed the bedside stories that I was told. I pretended that I, too, was a princess whom a brave prince would win for his bride. As I grew older

I saw the stories for what they truly were—fables to amuse children with—and realized that I didn't need a prince. But I still wanted a quest, a story of my own.

'I realize now that not all of us are born with stories. Only some are gifted with quests and are strong enough, cruel enough, to shape a story by themselves. For the rest of us there is only a chance to be part of their grand tale. And if we fail in that, we fail in everything, for nobody will remember us; they will only know the stories, and we will not have a place in them.'

'What does this have to do with Aresh?' the magistrate's wife demanded.

'I could have been a part of Aresh's story, had he wished. I wanted to be, but he was selfish and cruel, and wouldn't let me,' Nisia said simply, her heartbreak clear in the flatness of her tone.

'Tell me your story,' the magistrate's wife said, gently this time, for hadn't she faced the same disregard, hadn't she been dealt the same blow?

'I visited Thakir when I was fifteen, in an entourage with my parents,' Nisia began.

I didn't realize it then, but now that I think about it, it's obvious that my parents wanted to present me to the Amir as a suitable match for his son. I was young then, just coming into my beauty and power, and I was greatly put out when my parents declared their intent to cart me off to the ends of the empire just when I was discovering what all the capital had to offer.

I complained endlessly on the journey, but after a while my words lost their power and it wasn't just because my parents ignored them. Thakir is a beautiful place, nestled in mountains and forests. I had never thought that I would find it so lovely. It took us a week to leave the city behind and I became used to doing many things by myself. We could only take a small number of retainers and servants with us, and this sudden independence, this ability to shape my own life was a delight I had never before experienced. I often rode outside the carriage, with the sun on my face and the wind in my hair. My mother worried and fussed, afraid that I'd hurt myself, or worse, be burned dark by the sun and lose my beauty, become nothing more than a better-dressed servant girl. My father would scold me, but more because he felt he had to than through any real objection.

I made the most of my unaccustomed freedom, and it must have been true that I looked nothing like a young lady that day when I first saw Barab and Aresh. We were almost at the main city and had stopped just outside. My mother had insisted that we needed half a day to prepare ourselves, and then a leisurely ride into the city so we wouldn't look like the godforsaken savages we seemed to have become. She had said this while looking pointedly at my father, and he grinned sheepishly and laughed in defeat.

It was evening when the two young men came riding into our camp. Their sudden entry startled the guards, who raised their pikes and nocked their arrows to their bows. Immediately the burlier of the two dismounted, with his sword drawn, and demanded, 'Who are you? By what right do you draw weapons against the Amir's son?'

He had such a strong air of command that our guards immediately lowered their weapons even though Father had said nothing. Our master-at-arms was clearly furious.

It was Aresh, gentle, golden Aresh, about whom I had heard so much, but who had still caught me unprepared for such magnificence, who said softly,

'Hold, Barab, these must be the guests that father spoke of.'

And because his beauty had addled my thoughts, because I was young, I said sarcastically, 'The welcome of Thakir is a wonder, indeed. We have only heard of it in Yasurat, but the reality exceeds our expectations.'

Barab only grunted in response, but Aresh smiled, and there was something in his eyes when he looked at me, an appreciation of my beauty or pleasure at my spirited response, which thrilled me.

'Ah, my lady,' he said, and bowed to us, from his saddle, 'we are only wayward children lost in the woods. How would we know how to welcome such exalted company as yours?'

He could have been laughing at us—no doubt he was—but so gently that I wanted to laugh along with him.

'How soon may we expect you at Thakir?' he asked, and when my father said that we wouldn't reach until the next afternoon, Aresh smiled wistfully and said, with laughter in his voice, 'Each hour we have to wait will be a sore penance that you have set us for this indiscretion. Don't punish us overmuch.'

His eyes were on me as he said the last words, and I knew that I was in love and that it was going to be all the great things people had said it was.

I was right for only half a day—an evening and a morning was all I had in the story that was Aresh.

Our first evening in Thakir was beautiful; we were treated like royalty. Aresh had dressed in the latest style to reach Thakir. It was already out of mode in Yasurat and I enjoyed making him blush. It was so easy to mock him, to push him and pull him at the same time, and it lasted late into the night.

The next morning my maid brought me flowers, and said that since Aresh had paid her handsomely to not tell me that they were from him, she wasn't going to tell me who they were from. We laughed heartily at that, and I thought of all the things that one thinks of at such times.

But during the afternoon, something changed. Aresh disappeared and I always found Barab in my path. I didn't understand.

It might have made sense if Barab had felt something for me, but it was obvious that he was also forced to be there. He wore fine clothes, but didn't care for them; he gave me flowers but he cared more for their beauty than mine. He looked like a wolf that had been given a bowl of lettuce to eat.

And behind it all, I knew, was Aresh.

I know what I saw in his eyes was true. Then why did the young man I loved send me his friend, who cared nothing for me?

I asked my maid. I asked my mother. I even thought to question my father but wept instead, crying myself to sleep at the evil in it all.

A week went by, and my father told the Amir that he had work in Yasurat. The Amir looked at his son; Aresh smiled, but there was nothing there. Barab smiled too, and it was as empty a grin. We rode back to Yasurat the next day.

'That was a long time ago,' Nisia said. 'When I heard that he had arrived in the city, I wanted so much to see him, but I denied myself the chance. And then he was imprisoned, and I denied myself again. But now he is dead, I couldn't deny myself this.

'I wasn't a part of his story; there is nothing in it for me. And though I bleed this day to acknowledge his beauty, it wasn't that which brought me here. I did not come because I was jealous of you, or because I wanted retribution.

'Even though I'm not a part of his story nor have one of my own, and my name is lost to the ages, I don't care. I loved him, and had to come because of that.'

The soft colours of twilight were gently melting into the night when the Begum ended her story. The pair rode back to the haveli in the moonlight, in silence. When they reached the stables the Begum gave instructions to the syce and the guards. She whispered to Mehrunnisa, and the maid came to the storyteller's side.

'The Begum will spend the evening in prayer, and asks if your comforts have been taken care of.'

'Enough, and more,' the storyteller said, clearing his throat to free the words. Sudden tears came to his eyes, as he surveyed the cold landscape. He didn't want to leave. How many hundreds of miles would he have to travel before he came to another house like this, before he found a woman who could speak to him in stories?

How long would it be, he wondered, until he knew warmth again? Before somebody gave him food, and it was love that he ate? How long?

His spirit quailed. He wanted to say something, to beg for mercy, become less than he was and follow the Begum when she left, to tell another story, to plead maybe . . .

It was a moment, and it passed.

'The household of the Mirza is generous, and gives more than it receives,' he bowed.

'Perhaps you will come by this way again when the Mirza is in residence,' the maid said, 'and experience the fullness of his generosity.'

The storyteller blinked, unsure if there was malice in the maid's words.

'Someday,' he lied.

From the corner of his eyes he saw the Begum shake her head. She would make her way to the zenana, now, and he turned too. Led by a guard, he returned for the last time to the haveli. He started to whistle as he walked.

He would sing, too, but maybe tomorrow, when he was on his way.

EPILOGUE

Many years after Rohillakhand, in Lucknow, where the storyteller's reputation was something of a legend, a young man came to visit him.

'My name is Mirza Ayaan Shams-ud-din Khan, son of Mirza Azeem Jalal-ud-din Khan,' the young man declared grandly. He had black eyes, and a moustache that he seemed very proud of, stroking it with one hand.

'I know nobody by this name,' the storyteller replied, his hauteur and arrogance undimmed by the years, maybe even a little sharper now that age exempted him from the normal rules of good manners.

The young man was nonplussed. 'Yet you stayed

with us on your journey out of Delhi,' the young man insisted.

'Where?'

'In Rohillakhand . . .' The young man began to explain, but the storyteller raised an imperious hand and stopped him.

'Turn your face so I can see your profile,' he demanded.

Uncertainly, the young man obeyed, lowering his hand from his face so that the storyteller could see the sharp cheekbones and the proud nose rising from his face.

'Yes,' the storyteller said, and after a moment repeated, 'Yes, your mother was kind to me.'

The young man bowed. 'It is she who said I should meet you.'

'Why?'

'She said there was a lesson you had learned, one I needed to hear.'

'About what?' the storyteller asked.

'About . . .' the young man faltered for a moment before raising his head sharply, in a gesture that was so completely his mother's that the storyteller saw her again, the glory of her eyes, the fire of her pride. 'About leaving your love,' the young man concluded, proudly and unwillingly.

'Then listen . . .'

After the leave-taking (the storyteller said) there is the leaving. And once you have left, you discover the ten thousand things that you still carry—memories of touch, scent and sight.

It is only after leaving that you discover the city within you has changed, and its roads wind now to different destinations. After the end of love there is the unloving, when you can engage in the ceaseless hunt for all those things to be taken out, and somehow discarded; when you can fight against the new roads and try, futilely, to return to what you were before.

There is, though, another choice. Half the story of love is the discovery of it as you put it behind you. And with that discovery comes the knowledge that your own journey is still incomplete. The maps have changed, the continents have shifted, and the horizons are not the ones you remember. However, the road is still open and there is much to see, but only if you have the courage to see that the first step is always a departure.

of friends, and the most honest of critics. Ouch. She also sent me a carton of cigarettes via her friend Anuya Upadhyay, to London, when I was editing and hoping, and in deep need of nicotine. Anuya suggested I contact Renuka Chatterjee, who, as my literary agent, has made getting a book published remarkably enjoyable.

At Penguin India, Ravi Singh made the extraordinary offer of publishing *The Storyteller's Tale* as a novella; something I didn't believe was even possible until then. I hope the gamble works. I am very grateful to Shatarupa Ghoshal, both for her keen eye and enthusiasm as she worked on the copy, as well as her politeness and courtesy. And Rachna Kalra—the first friend I made at Penguin.

Lastly I'd like to thank Ateeq bhaijaan and Apa. The rest of the world may have writing grants, scholarships and fellowships; I've been lucky to have an elder brother and a sister, long-suffering but ever generous.

ACKNOWLEDGEMENTS

The Storyteller's Tale started out as a retelling of the old stories I had heard as a child and contains elements of Indian, Quranic, Biblical and other tales. I was, of course, introduced to most of these stories and much of the poetry by my parents, although the fact that my Urdu is weak and Farsi non-existent has meant that they have always regarded me as something of a *jaahil*. Nadeem Suhrawardy helped with the historical research to compensate for my *jihaalat*, and I am indebted to him. I am also grateful to Michael and Plaxy Arthur under whose roof the first draft of this story was composed.

No person provided greater support for the writing than Sabah Hamid, who has been the most generous